The Tiara Club

at Ruby Mansions

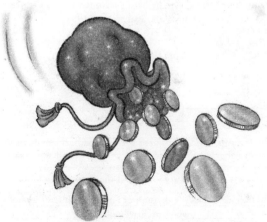

For darling Princess Maria xxx
VF

www.tiaraclub.co.uk

ORCHARD BOOKS
338 Euston Road, London NW1 3BH
Orchard Books Australia
Level 17/207 Kent St, Sydney, NSW 2000

A Paperback Original
First published in Great Britain in 2007
Text © Vivian French 2007
Cover illustration © Sarah Gibb 2007
Inside illustrations © Orchard Books 2007

A CIP catalogue record for this book is available
from the British Library.

ISBN 978 1 84616 294 7

1 3 5 7 9 10 8 6 4 2

Printed in Great Britain

The paper and board used in this paperback are natural
recyclable products made from wood grown in sustainable
forests. The manufacturing processes conform to the
environmental regulations of the country of origin.

Orchard Books is a division of Hachette Children's Books
www. orchardbooks.co.uk

The Tiara Club
at Ruby Mansions

Princess Lauren
and the Diamond Necklace

By Vivian French

ORCHARD BOOKS

The Royal Palace Academy
for the Preparation of Perfect Princesses

(Known to our students as "The Princess Academy")

OUR SCHOOL MOTTO:
*A Perfect Princess always thinks of others
before herself, and is kind, caring and truthful.*

Ruby Mansions offers a complete education for
Tiara Club princesses with emphasis on the
creative arts. The curriculum includes:

*Innovative Ideas for our
Friendship Festival*

*Ballet for Grace
and Poise*

*Designing Floral
Bouquets
(all thorns will be
removed)*

*A visit to the Diamond
Exhibition
(on the joyous occasion of
Queen Fabiola's birthday)*

Our headteacher, Queen Fabiola, is present at all times,
and students are well looked after by the head fairy
godmother, Fairy G, and her assistant, Fairy Angora.

Our resident staff and visiting experts include:

*KING BERNARDO IV
(Ruby Mansions Governor)*

*LADY HARRIS
(Secretary to Queen Fabiola)*

*LADY ARAMINTA
(Princess Academy Matron)*

*QUEEN MOTHER MATILDA
(Etiquette, Posture and
Flower Arranging)*

We award tiara points to encourage our Tiara Club princesses towards the next level. All princesses who win enough points at Ruby Mansions will attend a celebration ball, where they will be presented with their Ruby Sashes.

Ruby Sash Tiara Club princesses are invited to go on to Pearl Palace, our very special residence for Perfect Princesses, where they may continue their education at a higher level.

PLEASE NOTE:
Princesses are expected to arrive at
the Academy with a *minimum* of:

TWENTY BALLGOWNS
(with all necessary hoops,
petticoats, etc)

TWELVE DAY DRESSES

SEVEN GOWNS
suitable for garden parties,
and other special
day occasions

TWELVE TIARAS

DANCING SHOES
five pairs

VELVET SLIPPERS
three pairs

RIDING BOOTS
two pairs

Cloaks, muffs, stoles, gloves
and other essential
accessories as required

Greetings, dear princess!
I'm Lauren, by the way. And did
you know I'm a Poppy Room Princess?
Chloe, Jessica, Georgia, Olivia
and Amy are my very best friends, just
like you - and I'm so glad we're all at
Ruby Mansions together. Do you have
day trips in your school? We do, and
we have SUCH fun - just as long as
Diamonde and Gruella don't spoil
everything. You've met them, I'm sure.
They're the horrible twins...

Chapter One

We were SO excited! We were being taken to the Annual Exhibition of Dazzling Diamonds for Royalty, Peers and Princesses, and the coaches were lined up outside Ruby Mansions' front door. Lady Harris (that's our headteacher's secretary) was checking her lists as we came hurrying out of school.

"Poppy Room all together? That's excellent," she said as we skipped down the steps. "Please take coach number four. Hurry along now – Queen Fabiola doesn't want you to be late today of all days."

Chloe and I looked at each other in surprise. "Please, Lady Harris," I asked, "why is today special?"

Lady Harris shook her head at me. "Really, Princess Lauren!" she said. "I can tell YOU didn't check the notice board this morning.

It's Queen Fabiola's birthday! We go to the exhibition every year to celebrate, and there's a wonderful lunch party for the queen and her brother and her closest friends...and all of us are invited as well."

"That's lovely." Chloe looked most impressed.

"Is it just an exhibition," Georgia asked, "or can people buy things while they're there?"

There was the teeniest twinkle in Lady Harris's eyes as she answered. "Well...yes, you can buy things. Queen Fabiola's brother usually asks her to choose

something for her birthday, and
I suspect she quite enjoys that."

"WE'RE going to buy new
tiaras," said a voice behind us,
and Diamonde pushed rudely in
between Chloe and me. "Aren't
we, Gruella?"

Gruella waved a sweet little pink velvet bag in the air. "We certainly are," she agreed. "Mummy's sent us LOADS of money. She says we're to buy the BEST tiaras we can find! Come on, Diamonde." She pulled at her sister's arm, and they flounced off towards the first coach.

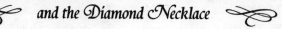

"Were we meant to bring money with us?" Jessica asked as we stared after them. "It didn't say we should on the noticeboard."

Lady Harris gave a little cough, and I SO had the feeling she didn't approve of the twins. But all she said was, "Queen Fabiola wants you to concentrate on the exhibition rather than buy things." She paused, and gave a wistful sigh. "There are some VERY beautiful crowns and tiaras... Now, into that coach, my dears."

We scurried across to the fourth coach. Alice and Daisy from Rose

Room were already inside, and they smiled at us.

"Hurrah!" Daisy clapped her hands. "We're so glad it's you!"

"We got split up from the other Rose Roomers," Alice said, "and we were scared stiff we'd end up sharing with Gruella and Diamonde."

Olivia made a face. "They rushed off to get in the first coach. They want to buy themselves tiaras."

Alice looked shocked. "Queen Fabiola won't like that very much. We're meant to be studying the exhibition so we don't mess up when we have our Royal Rules and Requirements lesson."

We all sat bolt upright. "Nobody told US about a lesson like that!" Georgia squeaked indignantly.

"Nobody told us either," Daisy said. "But Alice's big sister was here last year, and she warned Alice to pay attention."

Alice grinned. "My big sis got SO many minus tiara points! She just wandered round the exhibition thinking 'Oooh, lovely!' and then the next day she discovered she was meant to know EXACTLY what sort of tiara to wear to a christening!"

I pulled my notebook out of my bag. "Right," I said. "We're going to earn ourselves LOADS of tiara points. Has anyone got a pencil?"

Jessica waved one under my nose. "Here you are. And – hey! Maybe we'll actually get more points than Diamonde and Gruella!"

Chapter Two

The diamond exhibition was HUGE. I don't think any of us had expected there to be so many rooms, or that there would be so many soldiers on guard. Every room had dazzling displays of crowns and tiaras labelled *Perfect for Giving Away Prizes*, or *Perfect for Welcoming Foreign Officials*, or *Perfect for Encouraging Fairies To Give You Wishes*. There were hundreds of diamond bracelets and necklaces and earrings as well, and some of them were utterly gorgeous.

Alice and Daisy went off to join the others from Rose Room, and we started work immediately. Luckily Georgia's very good at drawing, so she drew pictures of all the different styles, and the rest of us took turns writing notes.

There was one FABULOUS diamond necklace that sparkled so brightly it almost made my eyes ache! I couldn't help giving a little sigh as we walked away from it into the next room.

We worked SO hard! We were just leaving the last room after making notes on the *Ideal First Tiara For Your Precious Royal Baby* when we saw Diamonde and Gruella coming towards us.

"Oh, DO look, Gruella!" Diamonde said with a horrible sneery smile. "It's the poor little Poppies! I don't suppose they've been able to buy ANYTHING.

Of course WE have, haven't we?"

Gruella nodded. She was carrying a fancy carrier bag, but she didn't look nearly as happy as Diamonde. "YOU bought something," she said. "There wasn't enough money left for poor little me!"

"Don't tell fibs! You've got a lovely ring!" Diamonde told her. "And you can wear my tiara when I'm not using it."

Gruella stuck her hand under my nose so I could see the tiny diamond ring on her finger. "Do YOU think that's fair, Lauren?" she asked. "Diamonde's got the most expensive tiara in the whole exhibition, and all I've got is this!"

"Erm..." I began, but before I could say anything else Diamonde cut in.

"Lauren agrees with me," she said. "Honestly – I don't know WHAT you're fussing about, Gruella!"

Now, I don't know about you, but I absolutely HATE it when someone's being unfair. And I don't like it when someone tells me what to think, either. I know Perfect Princesses are always supposed to be calm and graceful, but I'm not always very good at remembering in time to stop myself saying what I think. I turned on Diamonde, and I said, "Actually, I think Gruella's right. You should have shared the money equally. If the tiara you wanted was too expensive, you should have bought a cheaper one!"

Diamonde looked REALLY angry. She glared at me, and hissed. "Do you know what? It's none of your business, Princess Know-it-all Lauren! Just you wait! I'll make you sorry you said that..." And she gave me one final icy look and stormed off.

Gruella hesitated. "Thanks," she said, "but I'd better go and tell her I don't mind. She'll be horrible to me if I don't."

"Why don't you stand up for yourself?" I asked. "She'll only go on being mean if you let her."

Gruella shook her head. "You don't know what she's like," she said, and she hurried after her sister.

As we watched her go Amy said, "I feel sorry for Gruella sometimes. She isn't nearly as horrid as Diamonde."

"No," I said doubtfully. "But she never tries to stop her."

Chloe patted my arm. "Just be careful Diamonde doesn't think of something nasty to do to you. She hates being told she's not perfect."

"I'll be all right," I said cheerfully. "What can she possibly do here?"

Chapter Three

We decided we should go to the washroom to tidy ourselves before the birthday lunch, and we were just about to go through the swing doors when we saw the strangest little old king limping towards us as fast as he could go. He was trying to keep his cloak from under his feet with one hand – but just as he reached us he tripped and rolled over and over along the corridor. We hurried to try and help him, but every time he stood up he fell over again. In the end we untangled him from his cloak and propped him up on a chair against the wall, where he sat beaming at us with his crown slipping over one eye.

"Dear little princesses," he said, "how kind you are! But I think I'd better sit here for a moment until I feel stronger. All my fault for being in too much of a hurry."

"Can we get someone to look after you, Your Majesty?" Olivia asked.

"No, no, no," the old king said. "I'll be fine. Just fine. But perhaps you could do me a favour?"

We made our best curtsies. "We'd be pleased to help," I told him.

"Well..." the king fished in his pocket, and brought out a blue velvet bag that clinked as he waved it in the air. "I've just discovered I've got all this money with me, and no present. Could you dear girls choose something for my sister? I wanted to surprise her, you see, but I was late getting here...forgot where I was going, and went round in a circle by mistake."

"Oh!" Jessica's eyes opened wide. "Please, Your Majesty – are you Queen Fabiola's brother?"

The king smiled. "Knew you were clever little things the minute

I saw you. Know her, do you?"

"Oh YES, Your Majesty!" Georgia bobbed another curtsey. "She's our headteacher."

"Well I never!" The king's smile grew even wider. "Never imagined she'd grow up to do that, you know. Up to all kinds of tricks when she was young! But that was a long time ago...and now it's her eightieth birthday. Eighty years! D'you think you could find her something special for me?"

I had a sudden thought. "If you please, Your Majesty, we saw the most beautiful diamond necklace in one of the rooms."

"Just the job!" The king nodded so hard his crown fell off. "Run along, there's a good girl, and get the necklace for me."

"Certainly, Your Majesty," I said, and I took the bag from him. I was just about to go when the king picked up his crown and stared at it.

"That's very odd," he said. "Looks just like mine! Wonder where it could have come from?" He plopped it back on his head, and staggered to his feet. "Must find Queen Fabiola, my dears," he said. "It's her birthday today!" And he limped off along the corridor almost as fast as he had arrived.

Chapter Four

We stared at each other.

"Do you think he's all right?" Amy asked. "He seems very forgetful."

"My grandmother's like that," Chloe said. "But she's OK really."

"Lady Harris did tell us he was going to be here today." Georgia rubbed her nose thoughtfully.

"And that he always buys Queen Fabiola a present..."

I was looking in the king's velvet bag. "WOW!" I gasped. "There's LOADS of money here!"

"It's very nearly lunchtime," Jessica pointed out. "If we're going to get that necklace we'd better dash."

Olivia grabbed my hand. "Come on!" And we zoomed down the corridor – straight into Diamonde and Gruella. The blue velvet bag went flying, and gold pieces tumbled in all directions.

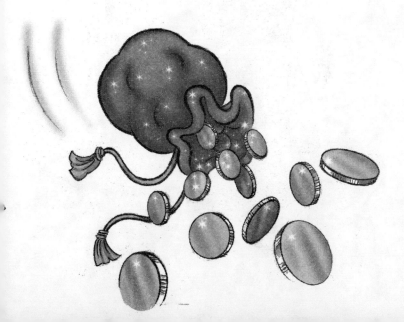

"Oh NO!" All six of us dived to pick them up. Diamonde and Gruella leant against the wall, and looked at us as if we were mad.

"Goodness me," Diamonde drawled. "Poppy Room have suddenly got rich! And they're

running in the opposite direction from the dining room...how strange. Gruella – come along. WE want to be on time!" And she swept Gruella away.

I didn't bother to call after them. I was too busy putting the gold pieces back in the velvet bag, and checking we hadn't missed any.

"I'm sure we've got them all," Olivia said comfortingly. "And isn't the necklace in that room over there?"

"Yes!" I heaved a sigh of relief. "Let's buy it, and then we can get back and go and have lunch."

The diamond necklace was SO

expensive! It took nearly all the gold pieces from the king's money bag.

"Do you think it's OK?" Chloe whispered as we watched the sales lady carefully arrange the necklace in a silk-lined box. "Seventy gold pieces is an awful lot of money..."

"The king did tell me to buy it," I said. "And I expect he could bring it back if we haven't got it quite right."

"That's true," Jessica agreed. "Although I think Queen Fabiola will absolutely love it."

We took the box, and put it in

the blue velvet bag with the few
remaining gold pieces. Then we

thanked the sales lady, and scurried in the direction of the exhibition hall's dining room. We arrived, panting, just in time to see Queen Fabiola stumping her way to the high table. Fairy G,

our lovely school fairy godmother, was just behind her, and several kings and queens as well.

"There's Queen Fabiola's brother!" Georgia hissed in my ear.

Georgia was quite right. The little old king was at the end of the procession, and the last to sit down. As soon as he was settled a trumpeter stood up and blew a loud TAN TARA TARA! and an important looking official in a gold coat marched into the middle of the hall.

"It is my great pleasure to wish Her Majesty Queen Fabiola, headteacher of Ruby Mansions, many happy returns on behalf of the Annual Exhibition of Dazzling Diamonds for Royalty, Peers and Princesses!" he announced.

Queen Fabiola waved her ear

trumpet in the air. "Thank you! Thank you!" she called, and we all clapped madly.

"And now," the official went on, "I call upon His Majesty King Forestino to make his

annual birthday speech!"

Our little old king jumped, and looked round in surprise. "Oh my goodness gracious me!" he said.

"If it isn't my sister's birthday AGAIN! Well, well, well. Of course I'm delighted to be here. Quite delighted. A very special birthday this time, eh, Fabby dear? Eighty years! Just fancy! And..." he began to feel in his pockets, "I've got you something a little different this time. Decided to surprise you just for a change. Nothing like a surprise! I've brought you eighty gold pieces for your birthday, dear sister – eighty golden pieces for eighty amazing years." The king stopped, and suddenly looked worried.

"Oh – OH OH!" His eyes positively popped as he pulled his pockets inside out. "Help! Help! HELP! I've been robbed! Robbed! ROBBED!"

Everyone gasped and we jumped to our feet and rushed forward. The soldiers stood to attention and frowned. Then Diamonde's high clear voice rang out.

"Ask Princess Lauren! SHE had a bag full of gold...and my sister and I saw her running away with it!"

Chapter Five

Have you ever had a whole room full of people staring and STARING at you in the most horribly suspicious way? It was DREADFUL – and it seemed to go on and on and ON, and I just couldn't speak or move. It was as if I was frozen in the middle of the worst nightmare I'd ever, ever had.

Then a voice beside me whispered, "Tell them, Lauren! That's SO not true!" and I saw Chloe frowning – and it was as if she'd broken some terrible spell. I gave myself a little shake and stood up, and my friends from Poppy Room stood up with me. My brain was whirling, and I knew I had to say something – but WHAT? How could I stand in front of all these people and tell our headteacher's brother he'd got totally muddled up?

"If you please," I began, and my voice was so wobbly I had to swallow and start again. "If

you please, I think there's been...
been some misunderstanding."
I curtsied to King Forestino.

"Your Majesty, it's true. I do have your money bag, but I also have the birthday gift you asked me to buy for Queen Fabiola. If I did wrong I'm very, very sorry, but—"

I had to stop. I was terrified I was going to cry, so I curtsied again and silently held out the blue velvet bag to the soldier standing right behind me. He clicked his heels together, and marched up to King Forestino. The little old king took the bag, and smiled.

"Very good," he said. "very good! All's well that ends well, eh?" And he stuffed the money bag back in his pocket, sat down, and beamed at everyone with the happiest smile.

There was an astonished pause, and then Queen Fabiola banged on the table with her ear trumpet. Her eyes were flashing, and I felt my stomach lurch horribly.

"Just one moment! I don't understand. I don't understand at all. Princess Lauren, what EXACTLY have you been doing? WHERE is my birthday present?"

I took a deep breath. "If you please, Your Majesty – it's in King Forestino's pocket."

And as I spoke I saw Fairy G give me a sharp look, and pull her sparkly wand out from her pocket. With a quick wave she sent stars swirling and whirling across the room until they settled on King Forestino's head and shoulders. He sneezed, and dusted himself down with a large purple handkerchief.

"What? What? What? Memory sparkles, eh? Who needs those? I remember everything – clear as a bell! Always do!" He put his hankie away, and produced the blue velvet bag with a flourish. He winked at me, and pulled out the box with the diamond necklace.

"Fabiola, my dear – Happy, Happy Birthday! One of your pretty princesses helped me buy this for your special birthday. Hope you like it."

I sank back in my chair with the hugest sigh of relief as Queen Fabiola began to open her present.

"She's just like us!" Georgia whispered. "She's SO excited!"

"And she LOVES the necklace!" Jessica added. "Look at her face! She's gone bright red!"

It was true. Our headteacher was absolutely glowing with excitement, and she gave King Forestino a huge hug just as soon as she'd fastened the sparkling necklace round her neck. He looked SO embarrassed.

"Think you should give my little helper a hug too," he said. "In fact, all of them. Six little princesses. Dear little things. You're doing a good job, Fabby – a very good job. Should be proud of yourself!"

Our headteacher nodded. "I am, Forestino, I am. Although…" she peered round until she saw Diamonde, "I didn't quite catch what you were shouting, Princess Diamonde? What was it?"

This time everyone looked at Diamonde. I expected her to look awkward, but she didn't. Not one bit. She smiled her best false smile, and said, "Excuse me, Your Majesty. I was just trying to be helpful." She turned to her sister. "Wasn't I, Gruella?"

And all of a sudden the most EXTRAORDINARY thing happened. Gruella said, "No you weren't. You wanted to get Lauren into trouble because she stood up for me! Lauren's NICE – not mean like you."

"What? I didn't hear that. What did you say?" Poor Queen Fabiola looked SO confused, but in an instant Fairy G was in the middle of the room.

"Thank you, Gruella," she

boomed. "But we don't want to spoil this lovely birthday party, do we? I think you and Diamonde should come and see me after lunch. But for now – I have a suggestion. Let's all sing 'Happy Birthday' to Queen Fabiola!"

And we did – and after we'd finished singing both Queen Fabiola and King Forestino came to thank me and everyone in Poppy Room.

"It's the most beautiful diamond necklace I've ever seen," our headteacher said. "And every time I wear it I shall think proudly of my wonderful princesses."

"Couldn't they have some of those tiara points you were telling me about?" King Forestino suggested.

"What an excellent idea!" Queen Fabiola said. "Twenty points each!"

We all curtsied gratefully.

"And now," King Forestino said, "let's have lunch! I'm HUNGRY!"

Chapter Six

The birthday lunch was delicious, and we all had a fabulous time. At the end there was a brilliant display of indoor fireworks – it was SUCH fun! It ended with a burst of golden sparkles that soared into the air and floated down, spelling out, "HAPPY BIRTHDAY QUEEN FABIOLA!"

And then musicians arrived, and the tables were cleared away, and we danced all afternoon.

By the time the carriages arrived to take us home we were exhausted. We collapsed on the soft velvet cushions and hardly said a word all the way back to Ruby Mansions.

That night we were so tired we fell into bed and hardly chatted at all, but it still took me a while to get to sleep. I lay thinking how lucky I was that I wasn't Gruella, with only a horrid sister for a friend. "Poor Gruella," I thought sleepily. "I'm SO lucky. I've got six LOVELY friends. Five from Poppy Room...and you. Six Perfect Princesses...and six Perfect Friends."

P.S. Did we come top in the Royal Rules and Regulations test?

YES! We earned another ten tiara points each. Diamonde came last ...but Gruella beat her by seven points, because she knew exactly what to give a queen for her eightieth birthday. A beautiful diamond necklace!

What happens next?
Find out in

Princess Amy

and the Golden Coach

Hello to all princesses – especially you!
I'm Princess Amy, from Poppy Room.
Don't you just LOVE being here at Ruby
Mansions? Although I'm sure Pearl Palace
will be HUGE fun – just as long as you're
there, and all my other friends from
Poppy Room too. I couldn't do without
Chloe, Jessica, Georgia, Olivia and
Lauren. I wonder if the horrible twins,
Diamonde and Gruella, will be at Pearl
Palace? Ooooh! They're SO mean!
Especially Diamonde...

The
Tiara
Club

Win a Tiara Club
Perfect Princess Prize!

Look for the secret word in mirror writing that is
hidden in a tiara in each of the Tiara Club books.
Each book has one word. Put together the six words
from books **13** to **18** to make a special Perfect
Princess sentence, then send it to us together with
20 words or more on why you like the Tiara Club
books. Each month, we will put the correct entries
in a draw and one lucky reader will receive a magical
Perfect Princess prize!

Send your Perfect Princess sentence,
at least 20 words on why you like the Tiara Club,
your name and your address on a postcard to:
THE TIARA CLUB COMPETITION,
Orchard Books, 338 Euston Road,
London, NW1 3BH

Australian readers should write to:
Hachette Children's Books,
Level 17/207 Kent Street, Sydney, NSW 2000.

Only one entry per child.
Final draw: 31 May 2008

Look out for

Butterfly Ball

with Princess Amy and Princess Olivia!
ISBN 978 1 84616 470 5

And look out for the Lily Room princesses in the Tiara Club at Pearl Palace:

Princess Hannah and the Little Black Kitten
Princess Isabella and the Snow-White Swan
Princess Lucy and the Precious Puppy
Princess Grace and the Golden Nightingale
Princess Ellie and the Enchanted Fawn
Princess Sarah and the Silver Swan

By Vivian French
Illustrated by Sarah Gibb
The Tiara Club

The Tiara Club at Silver Towers

The Tiara Club at Ruby Mansions

PRINCESS CHLOE		
AND THE **PRIMROSE PETTICOATS**	ISBN	978 1 84616 290 9
PRINCESS JESSICA		
AND THE **BEST-FRIEND BRACELET**	ISBN	978 I 84616 291 6
PRINCESS GEORGIA		
AND THE **SHIMMERING PEARL**	ISBN	978 1 84616 292 3
PRINCESS OLIVIA		
AND THE **VELVET CLOAK**	ISBN	978 1 84616 293 0
PRINCESS LAUREN		
AND THE **DIAMOND NECKLACE**	ISBN	978 1 84616 294 7
PRINCESS AMY		
AND THE **GOLDEN COACH**	ISBN	978 1 84616 295 4
CHRISTMAS WONDERLAND	ISBN	978 1 84616 296 1
BUTTERFLY BALL	ISBN	978 1 84616 470 5

All priced at £3.99.
Christmas Wonderland and *Butterfly Ball* are priced at £5.99.
The Tiara Club books are available from all good bookshops, or can be ordered direct
from the publisher: Orchard Books, PO BOX 29, Douglas IM99 IBQ.
Credit card orders please telephone 01624 836000 or fax 01624 837033 or visit our
website: www.wattspub.co.uk or e-mail: bookshop@enterprise.net for details.

To order please quote title, author, ISBN and your full name and address.
Cheques and postal orders should be made payable to 'Bookpost plc.'
Postage and packing is FREE within the UK
(overseas customers should add £2.00 per book).

Prices and availability are subject to change.

Check out

The
Tiara
Club

website at:

www.tiaraclub.co.uk

You'll find Perfect Princess games and fun
things to do, as well as news on the Tiara
Club and all your favourite princesses!